This Little Tiger book belongs to:

_____

_____

_____

To Roy, for help and sympathy
when the computer goes wrong!
~ C F

To Mum, Dad, Rach, Tim, Ange
and the rest of the back-up!
~ L H

LITTLE TIGER PRESS
1 The Coda Centre, 189 Munster Road, London SW6 6AW
www.littletiger.co.uk

First published in Great Britain 2005
This edition published 2016

A CIP catalogue record for this book is available from the British Library

Printed in China • LTP/1800/1725/1016

10 9 8 7 6 5 4 3 2 1

One Magical Morning

Claire Freedman
Louise Ho

LITTLE TIGER PRESS
London

In the shadowy woods,
one clear summer's morning,
Mummy took Little Bear
to see the day dawning.

The bears walked together
through grass drenched with dew.
Little Bear skipped,
as little bears do.

Little Bear gazed
as the sunrise unfurled.
"Up here," he cried,
"you can see the whole world!"

As the silvery moon
faded high in the sky,
Twinkle-eyed voles
came scurrying by.

And a little mouse gazed
as the morning sun
Melted the stars away,
one by one.

Fox cubs played while
the mist swirled like smoke,
Wrapping the trees
in its wispy cloak.

A pigeon coo-cooed
from a branch way up high.
Little Bear laughed,
"Look at me! Watch me fly!"

They stopped for a drink
at a babbling stream
And the sun turned the forest
soft pink, gold and green.

Bushy-tailed squirrels
scampered down trees,
Hunting for pine cones
hidden by leaves.

"Look, Mummy!" cried
Little Bear in delight.
As a mole burst, blinking,
into the light.

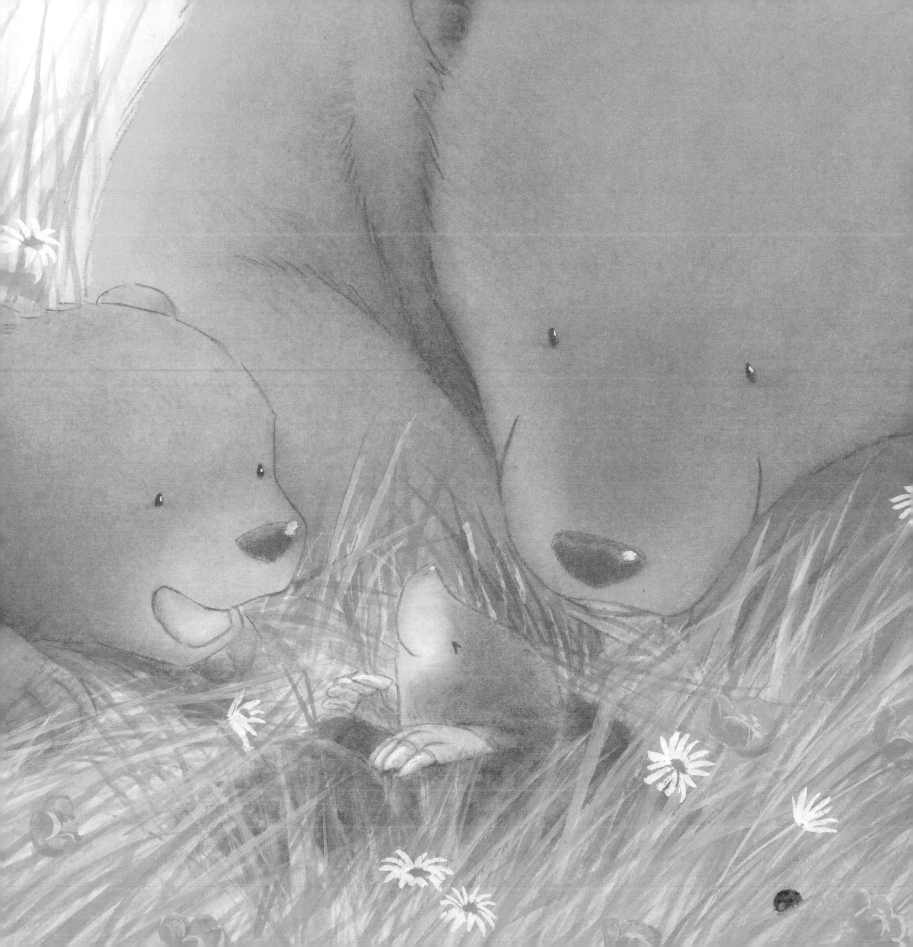

Mummy Bear smiled,
"Over here, take a peep!"
Bear's friend, Little Rabbit,
lay curled up asleep.

"Wake up, Little Rabbit,
come and play in the sun.
It's a beautiful day –
and it's just begun!"

More fabulous books from Little Tiger Press!

Bright Stanley
Matt Buckingham

Bored Bill
Liz Pichon

Rhino's Great BIG Itch!
Natalie Chivers

Ouch!
Ragnhild Scamell   Michael Terry

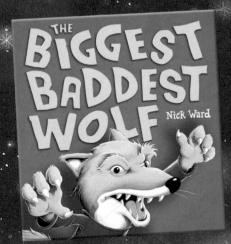

THE BIGGEST BADDEST WOLF
Nick Ward

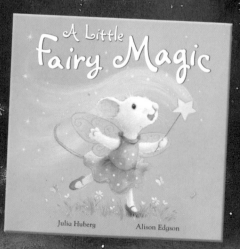

A Little Fairy Magic
Julia Hubery   Alison Edgson

For information regarding any of the above titles or for our catalogue, please contact us:

Little Tiger Press, 1 The Coda Centre, 189 Munster Road, London SW6 6AW

Tel: 020 7385 6333 • E-mail: contact@littletiger.co.uk • www.littletiger.co.uk